⋆ CONTENTS ⋆

★ Stone Soup ★

There was once a man, who met a man, who told him this story. He told it to me and now I shall tell it to you.

One night a poor tramp was travelling near a king's palace. Cold and hungry, he knocked on the kitchen door, hoping for a few scraps.

The cook was the kind of woman who sends beggars off with a few hard words and a rolling pin.

But for some reason (perhaps he had the right kind of smile) she said to the tramp, "You can come in, if you like, but don't expect any food. You'll get nothing for nothing in this house."

At first the cook kept her mean little eye on the tramp, but she was so busy she soon forgot he was there. The tramp sat quietly enjoying the cooking smells, glad to be out of the cold.

But next thing, there he was, by her side, lifting pan lids and shaking his head.

"And what would you know of cooking?" snapped the cook.

The old man smiled. "I know a good cook when I see one."

The cook grunted.

"And I'll bet such a good cook knows how to make stone soup." The tramp took from his pocket a long, flat, smooth stone and stroked it gently.

"Stone soup?" said the cook.
"Stone soup! Soup made from a
stone?"

"Oh, not just any stone," said
the old man. "It has to be a tasty
one, like this one. I'll show you, if
you like."

The cook's greedy eyes flashed. She liked the idea of something for nothing. "Bring him a pot," she shouted. "Fill it with water."

The kitchen boy came running. He built up the fire and put the pot over the flame.

The tramp dropped in the stone, with a loud plop! He added some salt, then he began to stir.

He sniffed the soup,

he sipped the soup,

he swallowed it down.

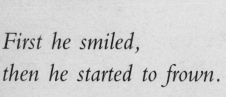

First he smiled,
then he started to frown.

"This soup *would be* fit for a king, if only it had one more thing," said the tramp, looking thoughtful. "An onion! That's what it needs."

The cook called the kitchen boy, the kitchen boy came running. Into the pot went a large fresh onion, finely chopped.

The tramp nodded and stirred the soup, while the cook kept her mean little eye on him.

He sniffed the soup,
  he sipped the soup,
    he swallowed it down.
First he smiled,
  then he started to frown.

"This soup is *not quite* fit for a king. It still needs one more thing." The tramp scratched his head. "A carrot!" he said.

The cook called the kitchen boy,
the kitchen boy came running,
and into the pot went two juicy
carrots, thinly sliced. The old man
stirred again.

He sniffed the soup,
  he sipped the soup,
    he swallowed it down.
First he smiled,
  then he started to frown.

"This soup is *nearly* fit for a king." The tramp looked around him. "It only needs one more thing. A handful of barley! That would do the job."

The cook nodded. The kitchen boy brought the jar of barley and the tramp threw in three big handfuls. He stirred the soup again. Then...

He sniffed the soup,
        he sipped the soup,
                he swallowed it down.
First he smiled,
        then he started to frown.

"This soup is *almost* fit for a king. It only needs..." The tramp shook his head. "No, never mind."
"What? What!" said the cook.

"A ham bone?" The tramp didn't sound very hopeful. "Just a little one."

This time the cook herself brought a huge ham bone, still covered with meat, and dropped it in. The smell of the soup filled the kitchen. The kitchen boy dribbled and drooled; the cook licked her lips. They both watched the tramp.

He sniffed the soup,
> he sipped the soup,
>> he swallowed it down.
First he smiled,
> then he started to frown.

"This soup is *absolutely* fit for a king. It only needs..."
Now it was the cook's turn to frown.

"A few herbs…"
said the tramp
quickly. The
kitchen boy
ran for the herbs
without being told.

"And a little
cream…" The
boy raced to
the larder and
brought a jug.

"A dash of wine
would finish it
off nicely."
The cook threw
in half a bottle.

The soup bubbled up rich and thick. The smells were *heavenly*. The tramp gave it a final stir.

Then…

He sniffed the soup.
He sipped the soup.
He ooohed.
He errred.
He almost purred.

The cook and the kitchen boy
watched and held their breath.

"And now," said the tramp, "without another single thing, this soup is...*too good* for a king."

The cook's greedy face broke into a grin.

"Fetch two bowls," she yelled. "And a loaf."

"And the rest of the wine?" suggested the tramp.

The kitchen boy ran backwards and forwards while the cook laid the table. It looked fit for a royal couple.

The tramp and the cook sat down and picked up their spoons. They sniffed the soup, they sipped the soup, they swallowed it down, bowl after bowl after bowl. Until they'd eaten the lot.

The cook leaned back in her chair. "And to think," she said, "it all came from a stone. It's nothing short of a miracle."

Before he left, the tramp gave the cook the stone to keep. The silly woman was so pleased she almost cried.

"God bless you," she said, "for teaching me to make such wonderful soup."

The tramp went on his way
with a full stomach. But as he
went along, he thought to himself,
a full stomach's soon empty. So,
he kept his eyes open for a likely-
looking stone.

It couldn't be just any stone, of course. It had to be long, flat, smooth, and full of flavour.

Anyway, that's the way I heard it, and now you've heard it too.

So... Snip! Snap! Snout!
This tale's told out!

★ Pancakes and Pies ★

Long, long ago, when times were hard, there was an old man and his wife who were so poor they had nothing to eat. Not even a bit of bread. So they lived on acorns. That's all. Every day they went into the woods to collect them for their supper.

One day, an acorn rolled off the table and fell through a crack in the floor. After a while the acorn began to grow. It grew into a tiny oak tree that pushed its way between the floorboards. "Husband," said the old woman, "why not cut a hole in the floor so the tree can keep on growing? Then we can pick acorns at home. We won't need to go into the woods."

So the old man cut a hole in the
floor and the oak tree grew and
grew and grew until it reached
the roof.

"Husband," said the old woman, "why not cut a hole in the roof so the tree can grow right up into the sky? Then we shall have as many acorns as we want."

So the
old man
cut a hole
in the roof
and the
tree grew
and grew
and grew
until it
reached right
to the sky and
the old couple had
all the acorns they wanted.

But nothing lasts for ever. Soon they had eaten all the acorns they could reach.

So the old man took a sack and climbed the tree right to the top.

When he could climb no further, he stepped off and walked across the sky. As he walked along he met a little cock with a golden comb. Beside the cock was a handmill.

The old man didn't like to go home empty-handed, so he put the cock and the handmill into his sack and climbed back down the tree.

 "Well, where's the supper?" asked the old woman.

The old man emptied the sack. There were no acorns, just the cock with the golden comb and the handmill. The old woman didn't know what to think. But she picked up the handmill and turned the handle. What a surprise!

Out of the mill came
    pancakes and pies!
Pancakes and pies!
    More pancakes and pies!
The old couple could hardly
    believe their own eyes.
A stream! A river
    of pancakes and pies.

Well, they were never hungry after that. If it was pancakes for breakfast, it was pies for supper. A different sort every day. The old man and the old woman and the little cock with the golden comb grew fat and happy.

But even good luck doesn't last
for ever. One day the king came
riding by. He was a greedy man
and he hadn't eaten for at least
half an hour.

"Old woman," he called, "I'm
hungry. What have you got for
me to eat?"

"Well, sire, I can only give you
pancakes or pies."

"That will do very well," said
the king.

He tied up his horse and went into the cottage. The old woman turned her handmill and out poured a stream of pancakes and pies. The greedy king gobbled up a dozen of each. They were the best pancakes and pies he'd ever tasted.

"I want to buy that handmill," he said. "How much do you want for it?"

"Oh, we couldn't sell it, sire," said the old woman. "Not for all the money in the world."

But no one says no to a king. He just took it. He rode off on his horse, with the handmill under his arm. You should have heard the crying. The old man wept and the old woman wailed. But what could they do? You can't argue with a king.

Then the little cock jumped up.
"Don't worry," he told the old
couple. "I'll bring back our
handmill."

He flew and he flew until he reached the king's palace. He landed on the roof and crowed:

"Cock-er-ick-oo!
What shall we do?
The king stole our mill,
And he has it still."

When the king heard the cock
he was furious. He told his
servants, "Catch that cock and
throw him down the well."

So the servants caught the little cock and threw him down the well. But did the cock care? No, he did not. This is what he said:

"*Little beak, clever beak,*
Drink up the water.
Please don't stop,
Till you've drunk the last drop."

His little beak drank until the
well was dry and the cock flew
out. This time he landed outside
the king's window and crowed:

> *"Cock-er-ick-oo!*
> *What shall we do?*
> *The king stole our mill,*
> *And he has it still."*

When the king heard the cock again he was boiling mad. He told his servants, "Catch that cock and throw him in the stove."

The servants caught the little cock and threw him in the stove. But did the cock care? No, he did not. This is what he said:

"Little beak, clever beak,
Pour out the water.
Pour like a spout,
Until the fire's out."

His beak poured like a spout
and the fire was soon out.

Then the cock flew into the king's grand hall. The room was full of the king's guests. They had come for a feast. The king was turning the handle of the little handmill and pancakes and pies were pouring out.

The little cock with the golden comb landed on the king's table. He stretched himself up and crowed:

"*Cock-er-ick-oo!*
What shall we do?
The king stole our mill,
And he has it still."

The guests were afraid of the
little cock who could talk and the
handmill that could turn out food,
and they ran off screaming.

The king ran after them, trying
to persuade them to come back.
But would they? No, they
certainly would not.

Then the cock picked up the handmill and flew home with it. And the old man and the old woman and the cock with the golden comb all grew fat and lived happily ever after.

The old couple could hardly
believe their own eyes.
So from that day to this,
it was pancakes and pies.

Pancakes with syrup
and hot, crusty pies.
Pies and pancakes!
Pancakes and pies!

Stone Soup is a very popular story which comes from
Scandinavia (where it is called *Nail Soup*) and Russia
(where it is called *Axe Soup*). *Pancakes and Pies*
is not so well known and also comes from Russia.

Here are some more stories you might like to read:

About Food and Magic:

The Magic Porridge Pot
from *The Orchard Book of Nursery Stories*
by Sophie Windham
(Orchard Books)

The Girl Who Loved Food
from *Tales of Amazing Maidens*
by Pomme Clayton
(Orchard Books)

About Tricks and Tricksters:

The Barefoot Book of Trickster Tales
by Richard Walker
(Barefoot Books)

The Emperor's New Clothes
from *Stories from Hans Andersen*
by Andrew Matthews
(Orchard Books)

The Pot of Gold
from *The Orchard Book of
Irish Fairy Tales and Legends*
by Una Leavy
(Orchard Books)